An Old Soul's Journey

Chris Wasko

Illustrated by: Sarah Hameed

Balboa Press books may be ordered through booksellers or by contacting:

Balboa Press
A Division of Hay House
1663 Liberty Drive
Bloomington, IN 47403
www.balboapress.com
844-682-1282

Interior Image Credit: Sarah Hameed

ISBN: 979-8-7652-5261-1 (sc)
ISBN: 979-8-7652-5262-8 (e)

Print information available on the last page.

Balboa Press rev. date: 05/24/2024

BALBOA.PRESS
A DIVISION OF HAY HOUSE

Dear Old Soul,

Whether you discovered or were gifted this book, it was meant to find you. The journey of an old soul is unique and filled with challenges. These challenges will lead you to understand and learn more about yourself and your soul.

Your life experiences may overwhelm you at times. This book serves as a reminder that you are not alone, you are supported, and you are loved.

While designed as a children's book, this book is not only for children but is also for the child within you.

Thank you for being you and for being here. You matter and I am grateful to you for allowing me to be but a small part of your journey.

From my soul to yours, I send you love,

—Chris

Take a moment, Old Soul

And look up at the sky

Notice what is calling

Does something catch your eye?

You have an inner knowing

A wonder and deep care

Connecting to exploration and wonder

You are seeking something there

But what is there? And what is here?

Many questions lie within

Placing you on a spiritual journey

Are you ready to begin?

It's a journey for your soul

Something you have done before

Because, Old Soul, you are sensitive

You feel things at the core

Old souls choose difficult lessons

Have you noticed on your contract?

It's your agreement for each lifetime

That some might call a pact

You are learning through experiences

Lessons on love, loss, grief, and care

But do not forget about karma

It will make you more aware

Karma is for balance

Not to punish or inflict pain

While it does not always feel that way

There is much for the soul to gain

You are a soul first

And a body for a period of time

Molded together in the present

In a package of intricate design

You are the perfect human

For the lessons of your soul

Live, grow, learn, and love

That is the ultimate goal

Should there ever come a time

When this all feels too intense

Remind yourself, Old Soul

One day it will all make sense

Until that day arrives

Embrace the journey and the ride

For you are an amazing, beautiful soul

And we are cheering you on

from the other side

Love,

Your Soul Family

25

Printed in the United States
by Baker & Taylor Publisher Services